WARNING:

This notebook is the super-secret property of the

SUPER SECRET MONSTER PATROL!

The strongest, smartest, fastest (and only!) monster-fighting club in Stermont!

If you find this notebook, please return it to Alexander Bopp, 55 Jackdaw Street, before you're eaten by a monster.

The S.S.M.P. has been protecting people from growling, chomping, slithering, hissing, scratching, roaring, snapping, stinging, zapping, kid-eating monsters since, like, forever.

The S.S.M.P. has won tons of monster battles thanks to **4** super-secret things*:

1. Our awesome flag.

S.S.M.P.

DON'T GET EATEN!

2. Our awesome oath.

OFFICIAL S.S.M.P. OATH

RAISE YOUR LEFT HAND AND REPEAT.
(By moonlight, if you can stay up late enough.)

When googly-eyed monsters all covered in ooze
start swallowing school children whole,
I swear that I'll fight 'em (and try not to lose)
by joining this secret patrol.

(Nickname: SALAMANDER!)

3. Our awesome members.

ALEXANDER BOPP

Likes: Reading about monsters. Bike riding. Making battle plans.
Dislikes: Getting punched, chomped, zapped, or swallowed by monsters.
Fun Fact: Alexander's birthday is Feb. 29. (Leap Day!)

RIP BONKOWSKI

Likes: Sword-fighting. Stermont Stella. Cupcakes.
Dodgeball. Monster-bashing.
Dislikes: Veggies. Especially the kind that beat you up
and stuff you into a giant pumpkin.
Fun Fact: Rip's sleeves hide his amazing collection of
fake tattoos.

🍓 NIKKI HUBBARD

Likes: Strawberry gummy worms. Wearing her hoodie — HOOD. UP.
Dislikes: Silly rules that dopey grown-ups make up for no reason.
Fun Fact: Nikki is actually a monster! A good monster, called a jampire.
(See JAMPIRE monster info.)

🐰 DOTTIE ROGERS

Likes: Bunnies! Rabbits! Hares!
Dislikes: Getting hit with snowballs.
Fun Fact: Dottie's math grade has never
been lower than A+++

RETIRED FROM S.S.M.P. AT
8th BIRTHDAY PARTY
AT PUTTER'S COVE.

FORMER MEMBERS

🏔 JIMMY HOARSELY   RODNEY P[...]   📐 HELEN

Likes: Safety Land!
Dislikes: Danger. Trouble. Mice.
Fun Fact: Jimmy's hair stands
straight up — without hair gel!

4. Our awesome
monster notebook!
Which, obviously, you have,
since you're holding it.

(*Actually, there are FIVE super-secret things.
Turn the page to see #5. Our awesome headquarters!)

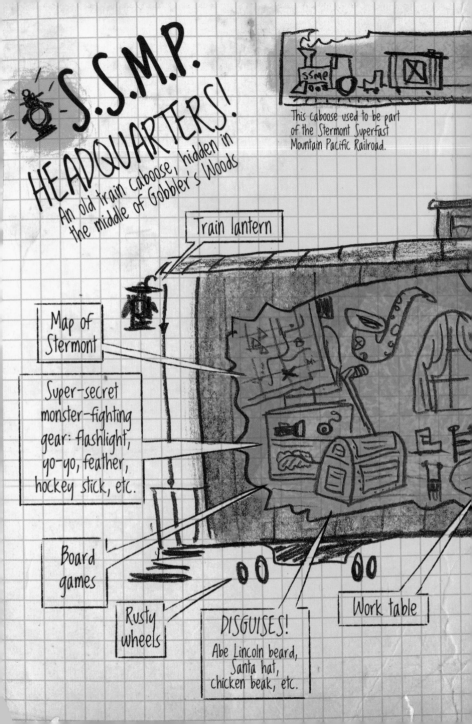

S.S.M.P. HEADQUARTERS!
An old train caboose, hidden in the middle of Gobbler's Woods

This caboose used to be part of the Stermont Superfast Mountain Pacific Railroad.

Train lantern

Map of Stermont

Super-secret monster-fighting gear: flashlight, yo-yo, feather, hockey stick, etc.

Board games

Rusty wheels

DISGUISES!
Abe Lincoln beard, Santa hat, chicken beak, etc.

Work table

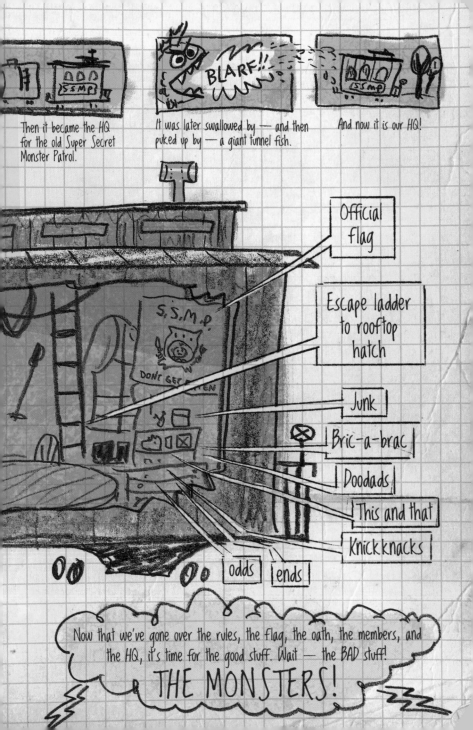

FORKUPINE

A small metal rodent
with a coat of tiny, sharp forks.

> HABITAT Most forkupines prefer dry climates. But the stainless-steel forkupine can be found near rivers, lakes, or in the back of dishwashers.

G~~ **CLANG!** Magnets will not work on forkupines.

DIET Mostly pickles and olives. They'll eat steak, but only if it's cut up into small bites.

BEHAVIOR The forkupine stays sharp by rubbing against a brick wall.

WARNING! Never pet a forkupine! Instead, lure it to a plate of spaghetti. (Forkupines LOVE rolling around in noodles!) This will give you time to sneak away.

FUN FACT The forkupine is a distant cousin to the sporkupine. But the sporkupine's scoop attack is no match for the forkupine's jab.

SABER-TOOTHED
SKUNK

Horrible, sharp, powerful teeth.
Horrible, sharp, powerful smell.

HABITAT The butcher shop.

DIET The butcher.

SWISH! saber-toothed skunks floss with jump ropes.

BEHAVIOR Each saber-toothed skunk has its own terrible odor.

STRIPE COLOR	SMELLS LIKE
white	burning tire
yellow	overflowing diaper
purple	shrimp smoothie from last week
green	buzzard burp
orange	pro-wrestler armpit
red	truck stop bathroom
rainbow	ALL OF THE ABOVE!

BUMBLE-BEAVER
Busy, busy monster.

HABITAT Old, hollow logs.

TIMBERRRR!

Bumble-beavers build dams that are 100 feet tall.

DIET Twigs dipped in honey.

BEHAVIOR These creatures buzz around the forest, smelling flowers and knocking down trees.

WARNING! Even if you dodge the bumble-beaver's stinger, you could still get slapped by its tail!

TUNNEL FISH

A creature that can "swim" underground. It drools A LOT, which loosens the dirt, making it easy to dig.

> SIDE EFFECT Tunnel-fish slobber makes night crawlers super smart, allowing them to read and write.

 **TEE-HEE!** Tunnel fish have ticklish tongues.

HABITAT Dirt, soil, mud. Not cement.

DIET Anything smaller than itself. When tunnel fish are near, worms flee to the sidewalks for safety. Tunnel fish will sleep for 99 years after a big meal.

WARNING! Don't get tunnel-fish drool on you — it's super-gross!

SPROING! Yaks-in-the-box get hungry when they hear "Pop Goes the Weasel."

BEHAVIOR This beast may wear a goofy hat, but it does not clown around.

WAR-NING! Don't turn the crank!

BARFALO

Ready...aim...upchuck!

HABITAT Parking lot carnivals, county fairs, and other places that serve bad food next to spinning rides.

BLECHH! The barfalo's distant cousin is the puke-aburra.

DIET Cinnamon rolls, fried baloney, grape soda, peanut butter fudge, sauerkraut, crabcakes, potato salad, cotton candy, hot wings, lemon shakes, cheese curds, hot dogs, and onion rings.

BEHAVIOR This monster eats all of the above, and then hops around on a pogo stick until its gut starts making a gooshy, burbling sound.

WARNING! There's no escaping what comes next. Just wear a raincoat, pack an umbrella, and hope for the best.

MANTA X-RAY
Invisible floating flat fish

HABITAT Any hard-to-reach place.
(Behind the television,
the top shelf of the
bookcase, under the
refrigerator.)

SPLORP! Manta x-ray slime is good for oiling a bike chain.

DIET Invisible floating cupcakes.

BEHAVIOR These monsters use their tails to pull pranks like:

Tying shoelaces together.

Unscrewing the pepper shaker.

Turning off lights.

WARNING! Manta x-rays leave a slime trail. Don't slip!

Who's a BIG BOY?

Come to a **birthday party** and find out!

WHERE? 55 Jackdaw St.

WHEN? Saturday morning!

WHY? To make new friends!

Hooray! Let's play!
IT'S GOPHER DAY!
Come celebrate the 1st DAY OF SPRING
in Stermont's sunny DERWOOD PARK
at HIGH NOON
See the one and only STERMONT STELLA!
OUTDOOR GAMES!
GIANT PRETZELS!
NORMAL-SIZED PRETZELS!
BRASS BAND!

MMMM! Violet fungus smells like peppermint.

BEHAVIOR These tiny purple mushrooms sprout on the heads of clobbered monsters, bringing them back to life.

DIET Old, rotten monster parts. Also: grape soda.

WARNING! A monster controlled by violet fungus is twice as strong, and half as nice, as a regular monster!

CHILL BILLY

Frosty monster that really gets your goat.

HABITAT Grocery store. (Freezer aisle.)

MEHH-EHH!

The chill billy's beard is made of sharp icicles!

BEHAVIOR The chill billy loves to butt grocery carts into the freezer case...

DIET Anything frozen: waffles, peas, fish sticks, and those little cans of concentrated orange juice.

WARNING! To stop the chill billy, get it to charge at you by waving a popsicle. Then dive out of the way. With any luck, it'll smash into the molasses shelf (aisle 9) and get stuck.

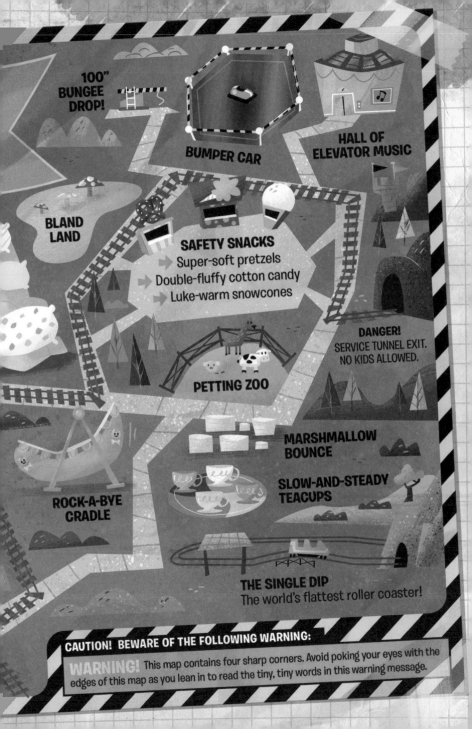

100" BUNGEE DROP!

BUMPER CAR

HALL OF ELEVATOR MUSIC

BLAND LAND

SAFETY SNACKS
- Super-soft pretzels
- Double-fluffy cotton candy
- Luke-warm snowcones

DANGER!
SERVICE TUNNEL EXIT.
NO KIDS ALLOWED.

PETTING ZOO

MARSHMALLOW BOUNCE

SLOW-AND-STEADY TEACUPS

ROCK-A-BYE CRADLE

THE SINGLE DIP
The world's flattest roller coaster!

CAUTION! BEWARE OF THE FOLLOWING WARNING:

WARNING! This map contains four sharp corners. Avoid poking your eyes with the edges of this map as you lean in to read the tiny, tiny words in this warning message.

SOCKTOPUS

A woven monster with eight mismatched arms.

HABITAT

Dresser drawers.
Hampers.
Gym bags.

DIET Sports socks.
knee-highs.
(No leg warmers.)

PEE-YEW! The stench of an unwashed socktopus can out-stink a skunk.

BEHAVIOR A socktopus is born when you forget to sort your socks. If you come across a single, unmatched sock, a socktopus is lurking nearby.

WARNING! The only way to stop a socktopus is to start wearing sandals.

RUST-BUSTER

Metal-eating monster.

HABITAT shipyards, iron mines, used-car lots.

WEE-OOH!
WEE-OOH! Rust-busters love to chase fire engines.

DIET Dishwashers, bulldozers, lawn mowers... Any kind of metal machine.

BEHAVIOR These monsters breathe a cloud of mist that causes metal to instantly rust.

Mmmm! Cinnamon!

WARNING! Rust-busters are allergic to wood. Hide in a tree house to be safe.

PSHHT! Mushy shrooms wear too much body spray.

HABITAT Fancy weddings and/or middle-school dances.

DIET These monsters feed on brainwaves by gazing longingly into your eyes.

BEHAVIOR Mushy shrooms will sing their terrible songs until:
a) you fall head-over-heels in love or
b) you fall heels-over-head out a second-story window.

WARNING! These monsters can get you in trouble by sneaking mushy love letters into other people's backpacks.

SQUEAK! The blubber-duckie's song makes kids cry.

BEHAVIOR Blubber-duckies float alongside regular bath toys, waiting to be squeezed.

WARNING! Don't squeeze 'em unless you're ready to become duck chow. To survive: never take a bath.

PURPLE SLURPER

Two arms. Two legs. 39 tongues.

HABITAT Under the dinner table.

PETER PICKER PIPED A PECK...
PEEPER PIPER PECKED A PEEP...
PICKLE PETER PEPPED A
These guys hate tongue twisters.

DIET Purple slurpers love to lick chocolate icing and melted popsicles off of people's faces.

BEHAVIOR

Drooling
Slobbering
Stamp-collecting

WARNING! Scrub your face at least once a week, or you might get licked!

BLUE-THORNED HONKFLOWER

Beautiful plant, ugly sound.

HABITAT Hiking trails.

DOODLE-DEE-DEE!

Honkflowers love clarinet music.

DIET The tears of people who can't stand its terrible noise.

BEHAVIOR This plant blows a foghorn sound when anything touches it.

WARNING! Watch your step! Avoid touching the ground when hiking.

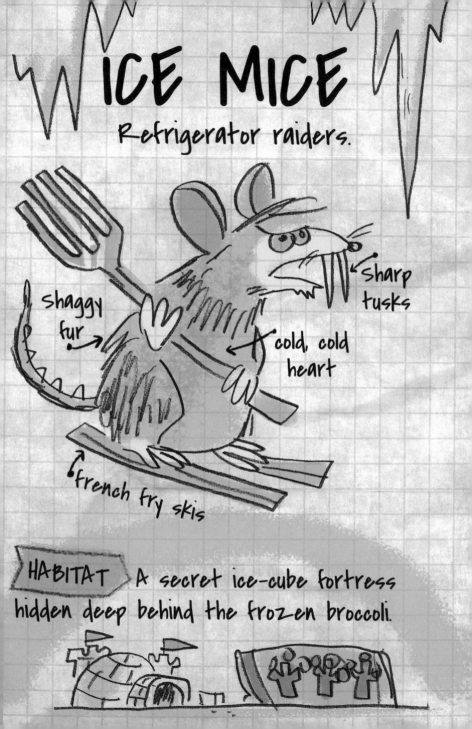

ICE MICE

Refrigerator raiders.

shaggy fur →

→ Sharp tusks

← cold, cold heart

↑ french fry skis

HABITAT A secret ice-cube fortress hidden deep behind the frozen broccoli.

EEK! Ice mice are sworn enemies of lava-cats, who dwell deep in the toaster oven.

DIET Cheese stolen from way down on the refrigerator's middle shelf.

BEHAVIOR These guys wait for the little light inside the fridge to go off— then they swoop down to nab the cheddar.

FUN FACT! Ice Mice rarely leave the fridge. But they do sneak out to steal cheese cubes from fancy dinner parties by hiding in giant frozen swan sculptures.

MEGAWORM

A small blue worm that seems harmless. At first.

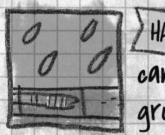

HABITAT Megaworms can be found on wet ground and sidewalks.

BEHAVIOR Megaworms always travel alone.

DIET Unknown. Possibly eats kids.

UH-OH

POP! Megaworms smell like caramel corn.

WARNING! A megaworm starts out tiny, but grows bigger than a school bus when sunlight hits it. Keep megaworms out of the sun!

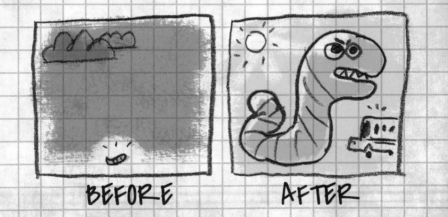

BEFORE   AFTER

WEAKNESS Any kind of loud screeching sound makes them shrivel up.

STICK FIGURE

Super-skinny monster that disguises itself as a flagpole, fishing rod, walking stick, etc.

HABITAT Rooms with high ceilings.

DIET Beef jerky and banana taffy, twisted into a long rope.

PECK-PECK! stick figures hate woodpeckers.

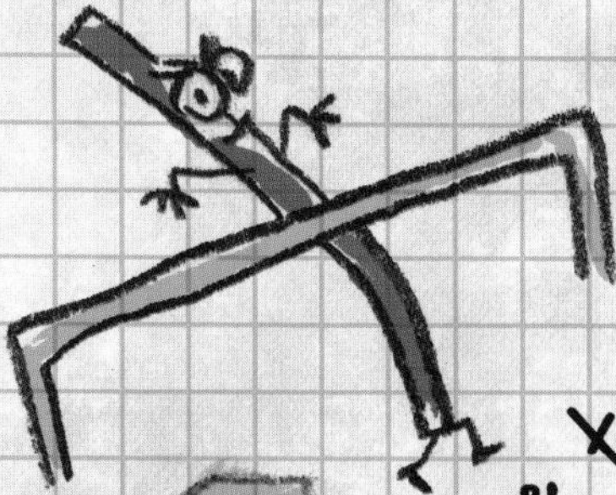

BEHAVIOR

These guys love to limbo.

WARNING! Stick figures can't stand water. A single drop scares them away.

KOALA-WALLA-KANGA-WOMBA-DINGO

Ears of a koala

Snout of a dingo

Claws of a wombat

Pouch of a kangaroo

Tail of a wallaby

HABITAT These monsters are found beneath the bathroom sink. Or below the couch cushions. Any place that's down under.

FLOOSH! Toilets flush counterclockwise when K.W.K.W.D.s are nearby.

DIET Boomerang-shaped food: bananas, croissants, squash, etc.

BEHAVIOR Koala-walla-kanga-womba-dingoes love to cuddle.

WARNING! It's a trap! As soon as you touch a koala-walla-kanga-womba-dingo, a joey will pop out of her pouch and nip your nose. Anyone bitten by a joey instantly becomes Australian.

Hi

CHOMP!

G'day!

CHEESE-BLASTER

No matter how you slice it, this three-headed ~~muenster~~ monster is up to no ~~gouda~~ good.

DIET Crackers!

HABITAT

unknown. But it probably vacations in Wisconsin.

TOOOOT! The hole-y Swiss cheese-blaster whistles when mice are near.

WARNING! This thing shoots molten cheese! Watch out for its three attacks:

NACHO CHEESE (Extra-spicy!)

COTTAGE CHEESE (Slippery!)

LIMBURGER BLAST (stink attack!)

GRATE NEWS!

If you can find a large enough slicer, this monster will be totally shredded!

TRAMPLE HAMSTER

Cute little critter with ENORMOUS feet!

HABITAT That strip of grass between the sidewalk and the street.

SHOE-IN! Trample hamsters wear a size 340.

DIET Anything flat and round. Pancakes, tortillas, baloney slices.

BEHAVIOR Trample hamsters love stomping things flat with their perfectly round, elephant feet.

WARNING! Trample hamsters dislike geese. Waddle around honking to avoid getting flattened.

P-REX
(Piñata-saurus Rex)

The P stands for "piñata," like the colorful paper container you bust open at your cousin's birthday party. Except this piñata is the size of a T-rex.

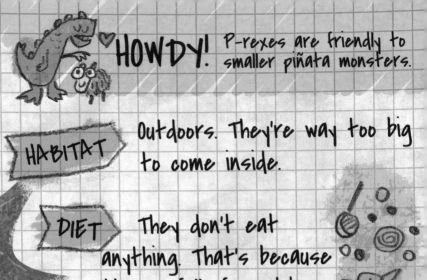

HOWDY! P-rexes are friendly to smaller piñata monsters.

HABITAT Outdoors. They're way too big to come inside.

DIET They don't eat anything. That's because they're full of candy!

BEHAVIOR P-rexes love smashing things. The bigger, the smashier!

WARNING! Whack a P-rex before it whacks you! Here's how:

1. Wear a blindfold and spin around three times.

2. Wallop the P-rex with a stick.

3. Watch it break open!

(PSSST! SWEET SURPRISE INSIDE!)

SKEETER-COPTER
Two-headed mosquito
with spinning blades.

HABITAT

Tents

Backyard
BBQs

Swimming
holes

HAMPER CLAM

Clothes encounter

DIET

Kids brave enough to dive down looking for a quarter, a candy bar, or a wadded-up spelling test in the pocket of the very bottommost pair of jeans.

HABITAT

The deepest, darkest depths of the laundry basket.

Hamper clams love to shred the toes of your socks.

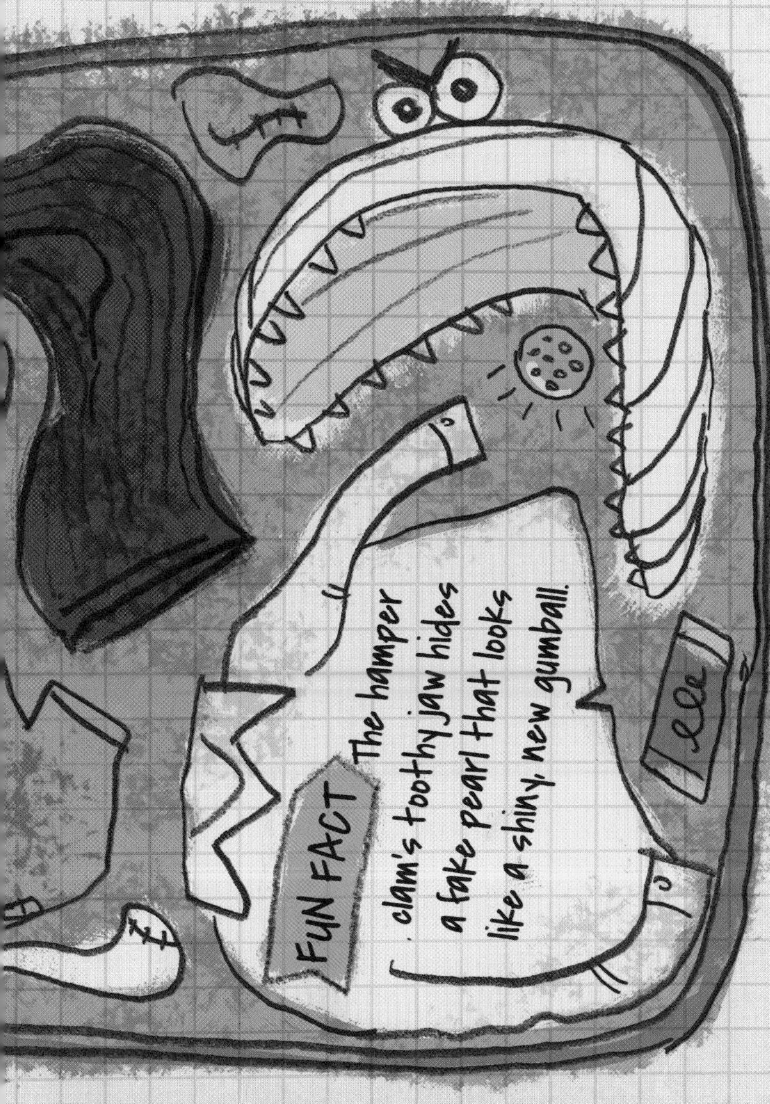

WARNING! Don't grab the pearl! Unless you want to be clam chow!

SKUNKY-MONKEY

A funky, punky monster that's
totally ~~stinky~~ stunk-y.

HABITAT — Clunky, junky old cars.
(In the trunk-y!)

SLAM DUNK-Y! These monsters think they're so hunky.

DIET Chunky, gunky old bananas.

BEHAVIOR

Skunky-monkeys slunk up tree trunks, where they plunk down hunks of gunk until you're sunk.

WARNING! A bottle of prune juice, when quickly drunk-y, will cause this beast to get all shrunk-y. Who would've thunk-y?

THREE-EYED GLOOMP

Not a lot is known about this creature. We're pretty sure it's green.

GOOD SQUINT!

Nearsighted 3.E.G.'s have a hard time finding glasses.

DIET Unknown. (Kids? Furniture? Frozen eggrolls dipped in caramel?)

HABITAT Abandoned buildings, most likely.

SIZE About six inches taller than you think.

WARNING! Umm... try not to get eaten. In fact, maybe cover yourself in rotten cabbage so you don't taste that good. Oh wait, three-eyed gloomps might like rotten cabbage. Look, just be careful out there, okay?

TRASH-SQUATCH

Walking heap of garbage.

Out at the curb, every Tuesday.

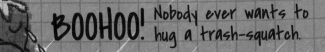

BOOHOO! Nobody ever wants to hug a trash-squatch.

DIET
Banana peels, rotten eggs, fuzzy bread.

BEHAVIOR
These monsters smell like gym socks filled with ham salad.

WARNING!
Trash-squatches are THE STINKIEST! Anyone touched by a trash-squatch must take three baths.

SKYSCRAPER-SCRAPER

50-story-tall snail, covered in spikes.

HABITAT

49-story-tall buildings.

DIET

Bricks, glass, and steel.

LAST! SLOWPOKE! Skyscraper-scrapers always come in last place.

BEHAVIOR This monster grinds its spiky shell against tall buildings. It eats whatever falls off.

WARNING!

Skyscraper-scrapers are only afraid of one thing: French chefs. Carry a spatula and say "BONJOUR" a lot to stay safe.

SUPER SECRET

CATWALK

LIGHTS

PULLEYS

STEP 1 | S.S.M.P. sneaks backstage before the assembly.

STEP 2 | Rip transforms into Monster-Rip. RAAWRRR!!

STEP 3 | Get Principal Vanderpants to come backstage.

CURTAIN

RARR!!

NOTE: This control panel pulls a cable that raises the curtain.

BLINKER

Your typical, everyday giant floating eyeball.

HABITAT Jewelry stores, car washes, clean bathrooms. Any place with lots of shiny, sparkly surfaces.

LOOK! Blinkers always win staring contests.

DIET They feed on light and color.

BEHAVIOR Blinkers love bad TV. Especially game shows.

WARNING! Never look them in the eye! A blinker's gaze hypnotizes you. This makes it so you cannot peel your eyes away from boring movies you've already seen 40 times.

PLAYING MANTIS

A huge green bug monster. About as
tall as a giraffe (minus the neck).

HABITAT All playgrounds — at schools,
public parks, etc.

SNIFF! Rainy days make the playing mantis sad.

DIET Regular-size bugs. (They spit out the shells.)

BEHAVIOR These giant bugs love playground equipment, but they play too rough. If you notice a dent in the slide or see a swing with one chain shorter than the other, then there's likely a mantis nearby.

WARNING! The only way to avoid a playing mantis is to sit quietly against the wall during recess.

HITTIN' MITTEN

They look cute, but they pack a punch.

HABITAT Glove compartments.

DIET Lint, fuzz, fur balls.

BOW-WOW! Hittin' mittens run when they see an arf-scarf.

BEHAVIOR These warm, fuzzy mittens turn into boxing gloves as soon as you put them on. Then: BAM! Stop hitting yourself! Stop hitting yourself!

WARNING! Hittin' mittens work in pairs. If you separate them, they become powerless.

POOL SHARK

Marco! Polo! Marco! Polo! Marco! CHOMP!

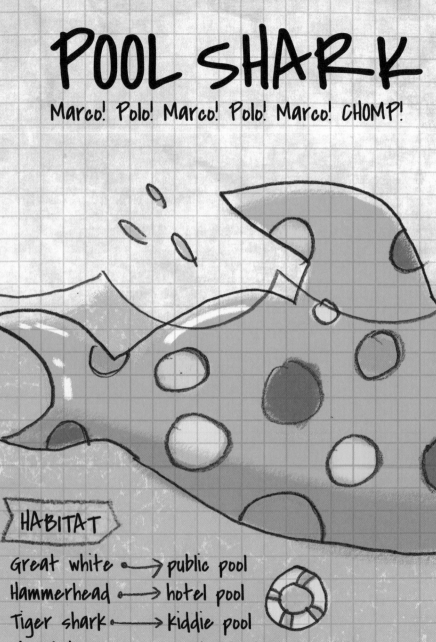

HABITAT

Great white ⟶ public pool

Hammerhead ⟶ hotel pool

Tiger shark ⟶ kiddie pool

Megalodon ⟶ Pool in the backyard of that popular kid two streets over.

FROG-GOBBLER

This thing eats 'til it croaks.

HABITAT

Swamps, ponds, fifth-grade nature walks.

PEEK!

Jampires have no shadows.

DIET Blood? Yuck! No! Anything red and juicy: ketchup, fruit punch, raspberry jam, jelly donuts, strawberry gummies.

BEHAVIOR Jampires are evil. friendly.

Also, they can see in the dark.

WARNING!

Keep jampires out of direct sunlight!

SNOMBIE
Snowman + zombie.

HABITAT Forest.

DIET Snowflakes?

EH?! Strange clinking noises seem to happen before a snombie attack.

BEHAVIOR These creatures roll along slowly, losing body parts as they move. They throw snowballs at anyone who crosses their paths.

WARNING! You can stop a snombie by knocking off its head.

CAMP

CAMP GLOAMY

CAMP RULES

Camp Rule #81
Always eat a hot breakfast.

Camp Rule #106
Don't make fun of beavers.

Camp Rule #44
Get a good night's sleep!

Camp Rule #3
If you step on a snake, apologize.

Camp Rule #114
Listen to your ranger.
He's smart as a moose!

Don't hum near beehives.
Camp Rule #299

ROPE
BRID

LOOKOUT
TOWER

CAMPFIRE CIRCLE

ARCHERY
RANGE

Camp Rule #315
Avoid going into a cave without a flashlight
and a book of knock-knock jokes.

ROCKODILE

Stone reptile.

HABITAT
Surrounded by things made of stone.

DIET
Aquarium sand.

BEHAVIOR

Good news: This monster won't eat you with its powerful jaws! Bad news: Instead, it will grind you into gravel. Just for fun.

WHAM!
The rockodile's sledgehammer tail can smash boulders.
FUN FACT!
The rockodile got its name because it loves the electric guitar.
WARNING!
You'd need heavy equipment—like a wrecking ball—to demolish a rockodile.

CUTTERFLY

Scissor-headed creature with paper wings

HABITAT Recycling bins.

DIET Coupons, paper-dolls, homemade valentines.

FUN FACT! Baby cutterflies look like safety scissors.

THE TERRIBLE, GIANT, POISONOUS, FLYING, ROARING, FLAMING, CHOMPING, NIGHTMARE-CREATING

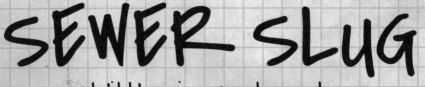

SEWER SLUG

sad little mis-named monster.

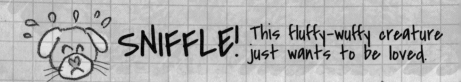

SNIFFLE!

This fluffy-wuffy creature just wants to be loved.

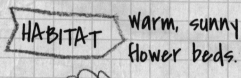

HABITAT Warm, sunny flower beds.

DIET Hot cocoa with heart-shaped marshmallows.

BEHAVIOR This monster is part puppy, part bunny, and part kitty-cat. It loves to play, snuggle, and purr.

SAD FACT!

Due to a paperwork error, this monster was given the wrong name. This causes people to avoid it at all costs. Which is too bad, because one nuzzle from this creature's cute widdle itty-bitty nose will heal your boo-boos and cause you to get straight A's in math.

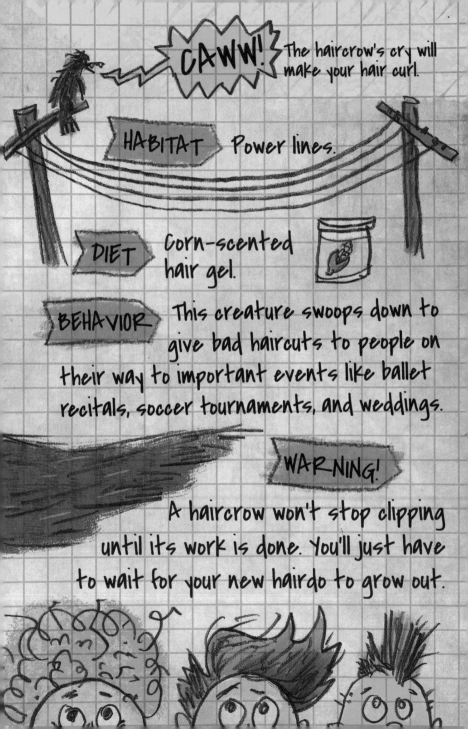

GRUMMM!

A whirly-wisp's growl sounds like a rumbling train.

> DIET

Jellied kid brains (served on crackers).

> BEHAVIOR

The whirly-wisp turns anything it touches to jelly.

> WARNING!

This monster will stop at nothing to eat your brains! But if you can draw a circle around it, the whirly-wisp will fade away.

SCREECH LEECH
A long purple three-eyed leech.

HABITAT

Found in closets. (They blend in with the belts and neckties.)

KOO-RAWWK!

A screech leech's cry sounds like a duck playing a broken kazoo.

> **DIET** Chipmunks.
Preferably with BBQ sauce.

> **BEHAVIOR** These bloodsuckers scream when they're hungry.

> **WARNING!** When you're near a closet, NEVER act like a chipmunk!

GURF! Mail manglers burp when they swallow love letters.

DIET These monsters snack on junk mail, but they prefer birthday cards from grandparents — especially if there's money inside!

BEHAVIOR Mail manglers just wait at the corner for people to walk right up and feed them!

WARNING! To beat this monster, send a powerful magnet to a friend. The mail mangler will swallow your package, and the magnet will yank out the mangler's bolts from the inside!

FUN FACT! A mail mangler's rural cousin is called a post-boxer.

KNIT-WIT

Yarn-headed monster with an ugly-sweater body and knitting-needle claws.

CLACKITY CLICK! knit-wits tap their claws right before they attack.

DIET Sheep! (Not the whole animal—just the wool off its back.)

HABITAT Yarn shops and sweater sales.

BEHAVIOR The knit-wit will poke you with its claws, hypnotize you with its ugly sweater pattern, and then knit you to a flagpole.

WARNING! If you find a bit of loose string, give it a tug. You'll either unravel a knit-wit, or totally make a kitten's day.

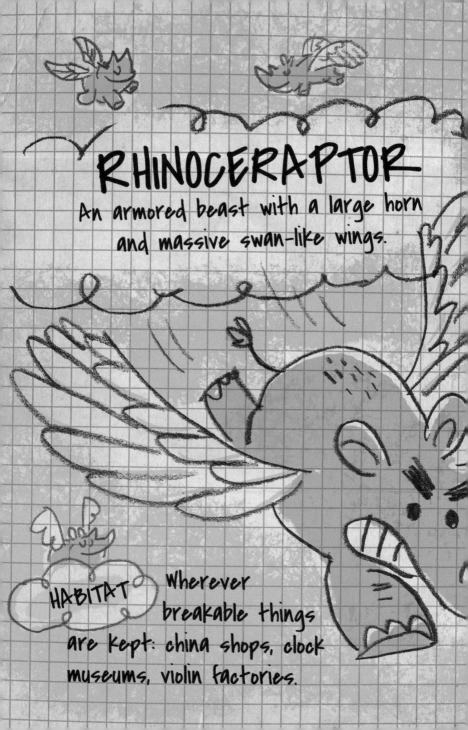

RHINOCERAPTOR

An armored beast with a large horn and massive swan-like wings.

HABITAT Wherever breakable things are kept: china shops, clock museums, violin factories.

YUK-YUK! Rhinoceraptor feathers are great for tickling your enemies.

> **DIET** Leafy plants. And corn dogs.

> **BEHAVIOR** These monsters enjoy a peaceful life in the clouds. But if they spot something breakable down below, they immediately dive-bomb their target!

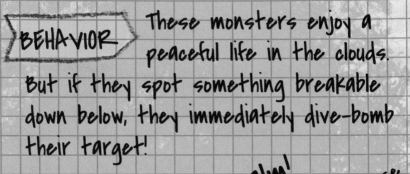

> **WARNING!** Stay calm! The rhinoceraptor can sense fear, so, SERIOUSLY, DON'T FREAK OUT!

The rhinoceraptor won't hurt you, but it'll gladly crush anything you care about—like a fishbowl, a sand castle, Mr. Nuzzle Bear, or a picture of your mom.

SPEWNICORN
Not-so-pretty pony

HABITAT

Magic rainbow castles. Actually, the port-a-potty behind a magic rainbow castle.

WEAKNESS

Spewnicorns gallop away when it's bath time!

BALLOON GOON

A tall, wiggly creature that is full of air. Most people pass right by these monsters without giving them a second glance.

Balloon goons dance in front of used-car lots, diners, and construction sites. They sometimes build balloon fortresses where they can hang out.

SIZE CHART

KID   GOON

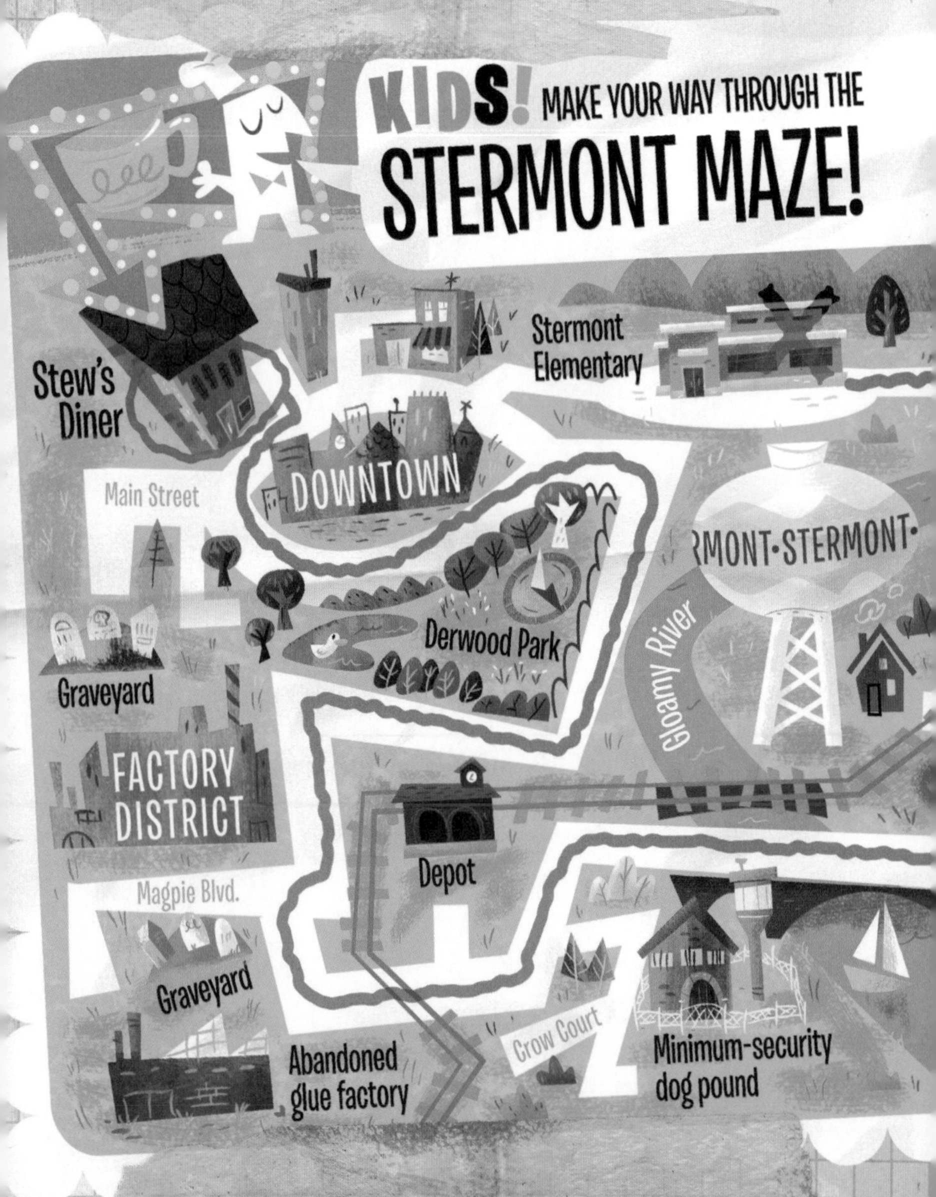
KIDS! MAKE YOUR WAY THROUGH THE
STERMONT MAZE!
Stermont
Elementary
Stew's
Diner
DOWNTOWN
Main Street
RMONT·STERMONT·
Derwood Park
Gloamy River
Graveyard
FACTORY
DISTRICT
Depot
Magpie Blvd.
Graveyard
Crow Court
Minimum-security
dog pound
Abandoned
glue factory

FISH-KABOB

A scaly monster with
a sword for a nose.

SILENCE! Fish-kabobs are bossy, especially to tunnel fish.

>HABITAT> Hospital laundry rooms?

>DIET> Tuna salad, from the smell of things.

>BEHAVIOR> Fish-kabobs are master ~~sword-fighters~~ fencers. They can unscrew their sword-noses to disguise themselves as regular people.

>WARNING!> Don't fight a fish-kabob unless you've had more than one fencing lesson!

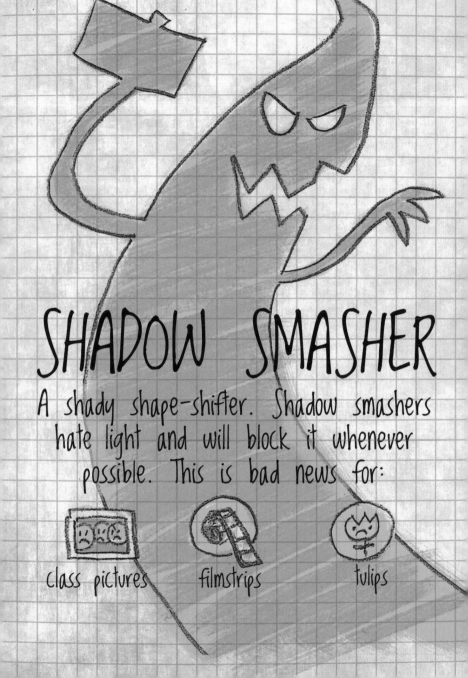

SHADOW SMASHER

A shady shape-shifter. Shadow smashers hate light and will block it whenever possible. This is bad news for:

class pictures   filmstrips   tulips

BRRRR! Shadow smashers bring a chill to the air.

HABITAT Right behind you.

DIET They "attach" to people and slowly eat their shadows.

BEHAVIOR Shadow smashers travel by jumping from shadow to shadow.

WARNING! Individual shadow smashers are silent. But put 'em together, and they **ROAR!**

YEAH, YEAH. Corn and tomatoes aren't technically vegetables, but we lumped them in here anyway.

BEHAVIOR Veggie monsters pretend to be school workers so they can chill, tenderize (mash you into shape!), and fatten you up before... CHOMP!

WARNING!

Got a beef with the veggie monsters? Cook your way out!

* Take a dozen mixed veggie monsters
* Chop into small bits
* Heat in a pot for 20 minutes
* YUM!

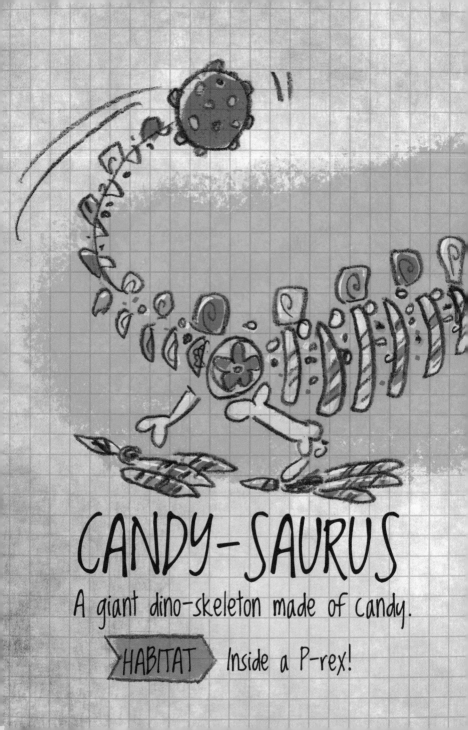

CANDY-SAURUS

A giant dino-skeleton made of candy.

HABITAT   Inside a P-rex!

BOOGIE!

Candy-sauruses dance when covered in ants.

DIET It doesn't eat much, but candy flies out of its mouth when it roars.

BEHAVIOR Smashy-smashy!

WARNING! Either end is trouble.

Taffy-blasting nose

Jawbreaker tail

PIP-PIP-POP! A bubble-wrap warrior would lose in a fight with a forkupine.

BEHAVIOR Bubble-wrap warriors like to steal treasure.

FUN FACT! These monsters are clever. They can turn a pile of shiny junk into a laser-blocking machine!

BEWARE! Bubble-wrap warriors can twist themselves into many shapes:

 mummy

 tornado

 octopus

 crawling hand

WARNING! If you find a sheet of bubble wrap, pop EVERY BUBBLE! Just to be safe.

ICE-CRUSHER

A huge blockhead who needs to chill out.

HABITAT

Gloamy Mountains.

DIET Frozen kid-pops.

(Hand-scooped by an army of snombies.)

CLINK! The ice-crusher creates snombies by clinking its fists together.

BEHAVIOR

This cold-hearted monster can make a blizzard on the hottest day.

WARNING! Fire cannot melt an ice-crusher! But 10,000 pinches of salt should do the trick!

THUNDERBUG

Power-hungry giant insect that
shoots electricity

HABITAT > Cocoon near
a power source.

DIET > Electricity stolen
from alarm clocks, escalators,
batteries, etc.

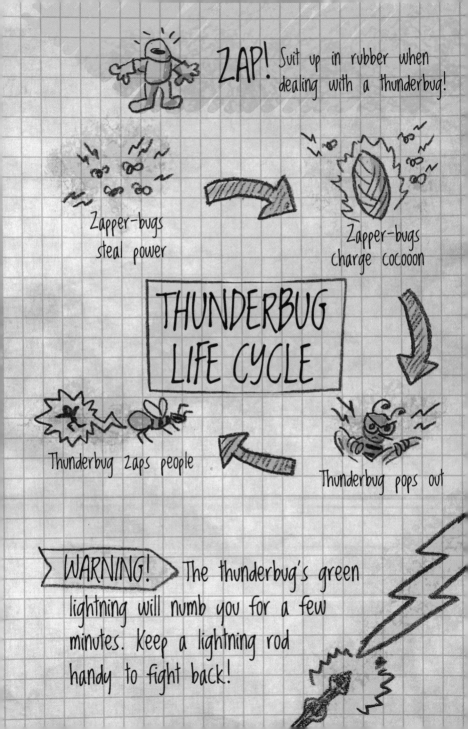

CRAB-RA CADABRA

Crab monster with a few tricks
up its sleeve.

HABITAT

Safety Land.

DIET

Cotton candy?

BEHAVIOR Pretends to be
a magician.

Fake glasses

Fake nose

Fake beard

Fake crystal ball

Fake sling

Real bunny!

SUPER-GOOP
Not-so-silly putty

HABITAT Stermont
Elementary School, ninth floor.

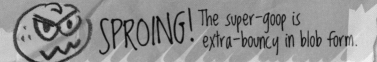 **SPROING!** The super-goop is extra-bouncy in blob form.

 DIET Lotion? Water? This monster soaks up moisture.

BEHAVIOR This blob can shape-shift into any animal/person/monster!

WARNING! YOUR teacher may be a super-goop! (Does he/she use hand lotion?)

KNUCKLE-FISTED PUNCH SMASHER

So so so so awesome!

HABITAT Awesome places like bike ramps, dodgeball tournaments, and monster truck rallies.

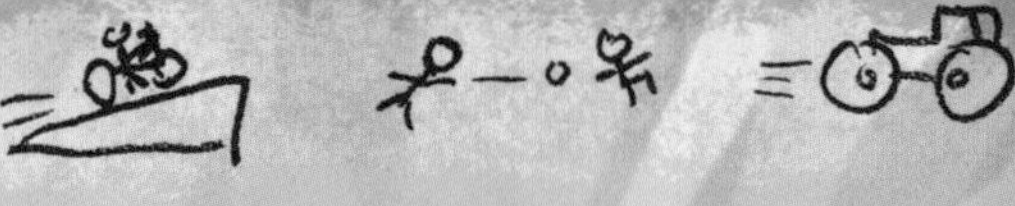

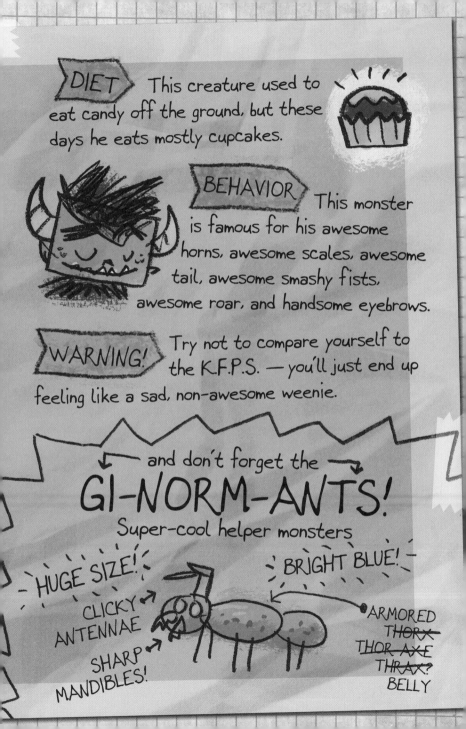

DIET This creature used to eat candy off the ground, but these days he eats mostly cupcakes.

BEHAVIOR This monster is famous for his awesome horns, awesome scales, awesome tail, awesome smashy fists, awesome roar, and handsome eyebrows.

WARNING! Try not to compare yourself to the K.F.P.S. — you'll just end up feeling like a sad, non-awesome weenie.

and don't forget the

GI-NORM-ANTS!

Super-cool helper monsters

- HUGE SIZE! -

- BRIGHT BLUE! -

CLICKY ANTENNAE →

SHARP MANDIBLES! →

•ARMORED ~~THORX~~ ~~THOR AXE~~ THRAX? BELLY

HMMM... This monster looks totally different with its hair up.

BEHAVIOR The nar-madillo has some powerful monster moves.

BALL SPIN!

HORN JAB!

SHELL BLOCK!

INCREDIBLE SWIMMER?

WARNING! The nar-madillo doesn't kid around. It's one of the toughest, most serious monsters in Stermont. Try to stay on its good side!

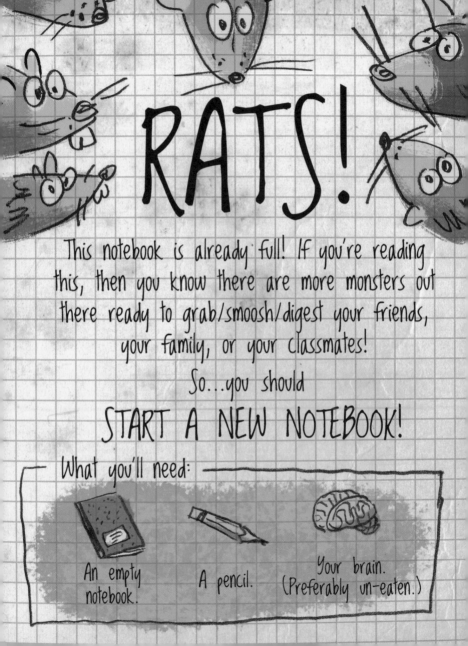

RATS!

This notebook is already full! If you're reading this, then you know there are more monsters out there ready to grab/smoosh/digest your friends, your family, or your classmates!

So...you should

START A NEW NOTEBOOK!

What you'll need:

An empty notebook.

A pencil.

Your brain. (Preferably un-eaten.)

STEP 1 Take the oath! (see p.2)

STEP 2 Stay on the lookout for monsters!
Walk around your home, your school, and your town.
LOOK for puddles of drool. LISTEN for growls.
SNIFF AROUND for horrible odors.
Monsters are everywhere.

STEP 3 Team up with your friends!
Grab a few of your funniest, smartest,
bravest pals at recess, and ask them to join.
Be sure to listen to their ideas, rely on their
skills, and trust that they'll tell you when
your shoes are untied.

STEP 4 Find your secret headquarters.
The twisty slide on the playground? Your
cousin's basement? The third row of your
minivan? Any place will do, as long as
you can talk without being snooped on
by you-know-whats.

KEEP OUT

S. S. M. P.

Good luck, and → DON'T GET EATEN!

BE CAREFUL! You may run across adults (teachers, coaches, babysitters) who don't believe in monsters. This could mean they ARE monsters!

TROY CUMMINGS
The dreaded, two-headed author/illustrator

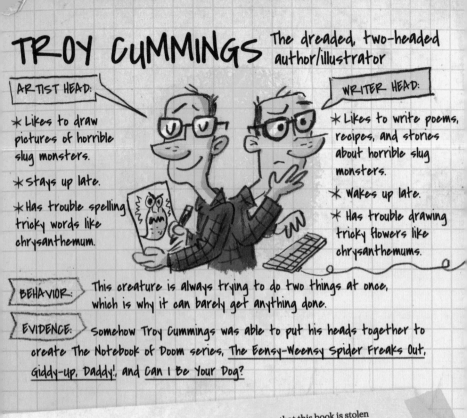

ARTIST HEAD:

* Likes to draw pictures of horrible slug monsters.

* Stays up late.

* Has trouble spelling tricky words like chrysanthemum.

WRITER HEAD:

* Likes to write poems, recipes, and stories about horrible slug monsters.

* Wakes up late.

* Has trouble drawing tricky flowers like chrysanthemums.

BEHAVIOR: This creature is always trying to do two things at once, which is why it can barely get anything done.

EVIDENCE: Somehow Troy Cummings was able to put his heads together to create The Notebook of Doom series, The Eensy-Weensy Spider Freaks Out, Giddy-up, Daddy!, and Can I Be Your Dog?

Copyright © 2017 by Troy Cummings

All rights reserved. Published by Scholastic Inc., *Publishers since 1920.* SCHOLASTIC, BRANCHES, and associated logos are trademarks and/or registered trademarks of Scholastic Inc.

The publisher does not have any control over and does not assume any responsibility for author or third-party websites or their content.

ISBN 978-1-338-15742-0

10 9 8 7 6 5

Printed in China

First edition, October 2017

Edited by Katie Carella